Elizabeth Imagined
an Iceberg

CHRIS RASCHKA

Orchard Books   New York

Orchard Books, 95 Madison Avenue, New York, NY 10016

Manufactured in the United States of America. Printed by Barton Press, Inc.
Bound by Horowitz/Rae. Book design by Mina Greenstein.
The text of this book is set in 18 point ITC Weidemann Medium. The illustrations are charcoal and oil reproduced in full color.

10 9 8 7 6 5 4 3 2 1

Library of Congress Cataloging-in-Publication Data
Raschka, Christopher. Elizabeth imagined an iceberg / by Chris Raschka.   p.   cm.
"A Richard Jackson book"—Half t.p.
Summary: By visualizing an iceberg and remembering how strong it can be, Elizabeth finds the inner strength to say, "Get away from me!" to a strange woman who is bothering her.
ISBN 0-531-06817-X   ISBN 0-531-08667-4 (lib. bdg.)
[1. Strangers—Fiction. 2. Self-confidence—Fiction.] I. Title. PZ7.R18148E1 1994
[E]—dc20   93-4875

for Lydie

Elizabeth imagined an iceberg
and, confident that it might be friendly,
she visited it often, quite bravely,
and told it to call her just Beth.

Now one day Elizabeth went riding
her bicycle, quite quickly, quite fast,

when suddenly a sound made her frightened,
so she slowed down, then tiptoed like a mouse.

Ahead of her breathed a large woman,
who looked like she might be six feet tall.

She seemed to be sipping some strange soda
and some strange soda it certainly was.

This soda was green and had bubbles.
This soda was green and blew sparks.
When the large woman drank it, she giggled.
She said, "Hot dog! This soda tastes good."

Just then Elizabeth ha-chooed.
Elizabeth ha-chooed again.

Elizabeth ha-chooed just loud enough
that the large woman heard her, and then

the large woman said, "Oh, how charming!
What a charming, pretty girl do I see.

"Come tell me your name. Tell it quickly!
Tell it loudly! And come sit by me."

Elizabeth answered, "Elizabeth."
But she did not go near.
It seemed to Elizabeth that somehow
something was not right.

Then the large woman loped and said gaily,
"The pretty girl is frightened of me!
I say! The pretty girl is frightened
of Madam Uff Da, the Queen of Bombay.

"Oh, I say! What fun we'll have together!
Just I and you, just we.
We'll fizz with the insects, we'll trot with the armadillos,
and we'll laugh HA HA HA HA HA all day."

Madam Uff Da Da giggled and giggled,
sipped her soda and giggled and coughed,

and hiccupped and laughed and giggled,
and laughed HA HA HA HA HA and coughed.

Then before Elizabeth could stop her

Madam Uff Da scooped Elizabeth in her arms.

And she danced and she danced and she danced

until Elizabeth felt very, very sick.

Now Elizabeth imagined her iceberg
and just what her iceberg might do.
Her iceberg would say, "Get away from me!"

So that's what Elizabeth did too.

Madam Uff Da was startled.
Madam Uff Da was speechless.
Madam Uff Da, Madam Uff Da
didn't know what to do.

So Madam Uff Da just stood there.
Madam Uff Da just mumbled,
"So it goes. What a shame.
Can't be helped. Hic, sigh."

Madam Uff Da watched Elizabeth pick up her bicycle
and Elizabeth bicycled away.

Madam Uff Da turned back to her soda.
Elizabeth did not wave good-bye.

Elizabeth imagined her iceberg
and remembered how strong it could be.
Elizabeth imagined her own self
and remembered how strong she could be.